Billy the Bullseye Butt Bull and Friends

DONALD C. KENDIG

THIS B⊚⊙K BEL⊙NGS T⊚

NAME

PICTURE
(draw or glue)

DEDICATION

To my girls: Savannah and Sierrah...
who never let me get away with just...
"Good Night!"

Yes Savannah and Sierrah. This is a chapter book.

CONTENTS

THANKS

Thank you Savannah. Thank you Sierrah. Thank you Lord
that my mind still works, and I can still have fun. Dear
mothers, fathers, sisters, brothers, sons and daughters;
Dear aunts and uncles, grandmas and grandpas; Dear
nieces and nephews, and cousins—sometimes several times
removed; Dear friends and family, and strangers too;
Thank you for your stories true— both fact and
fiction, serious and funny, and for play.

BRIEF INTRODUCTION

Contained within, you will find a series of short stories to read, or better yet, to be read to. Adults might find the stories funny, or they might not. Children of all ages should have a blast. Prepare yourself for the giggles and potty humor.

1

BILLY THE BULLSEYE BUTT BULL
FALLS D⊙WN

Once upon a time there was a bull named Billy. Billy was not like all the other bulls because he had a silly looking birthmark on his butt. This was no ordinary birthmark, though. It was in the shape— and color— of a red and white bullseye. Don't ask me why they call a bullseye, a bullseye, because it did not look anything like Billy's eye.

This birthmark is how, in first grade, Billy got his nickname. All the kids would call him Billy the Bullseye Butt Bull. Even the teacher would call him that.

Try saying Billy the Bullseye Butt Bull three times really fast:

Billy the Bullseye Butt Bull,

Billy the Bullseye Butt Bull,

Billy the Bullseye Butt Bull,

and I bet you will tie your tongue in a knot or it might stick out kind-a funny.

This birthmark was no fun for Billy, though. He didn't need a note on his back that said,

KICK ME!

It seemed natural that everyone would just kick his butt no matter what.

When Billy tried to play hide and seek everyone always saw his shiny red and white butt. If kicking his butt wasn't bad enough, his friends-- if that is what you can call them-- would throw balls, and marbles, and rocks at his butt.

Billy wasn't very good at sports and he was particularly bad at dodge ball because everyone had a great target to aim at. Even his teammates would throw a ball and tag him out.

It wasn't until 3rd grade that his friends discovered dart games. Darts are not allowed in first grade because they are oh so-o-o sharp!

To make matters worse, Billy was oh so clumsy. He had issues with gravity and he seemed to be always falling down.

There once was a time Billy was on a hill next to his home enjoying the view of the valley below when...

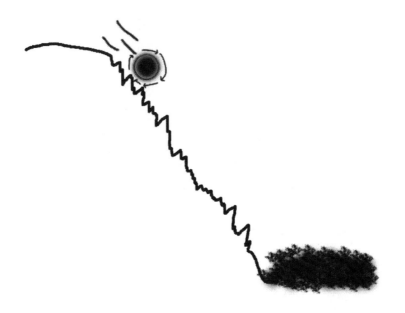

...Billy tripped on his right front hoof and down the hill Billy started to roll. The first thing Billy encountered were the sharp rocks.

As Billy rolled and bounced in pain, he saw his mom Marybelle the Bottomless Butt Bull. She's called that because she has no butt.

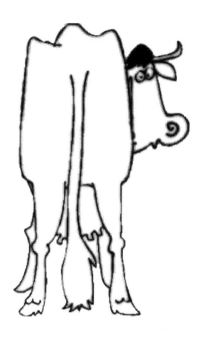

Really-- there's absolutely no bottom to her butt. It is flat as a pancake. O.K. Billy's dad, on the other hoof, had a huge butt, but more on that later.

Where was I? Oh. Yes. Billy. Billy is rolling down the hill and his mom Marybelle is walking up. Billy can't stop and rolls right past her as she looks at her poor son Billy with horror in her eyes because she remembers the rose bushes she planted at the bottom of the hill.

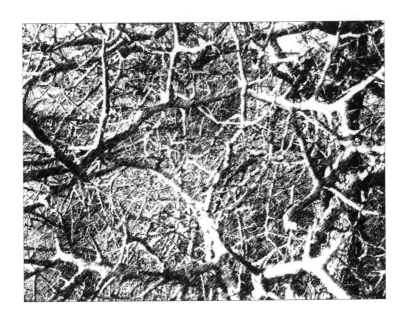

His eyes meets hers and he can see her terror and almost read her mind. Now he has a look of horror in his eyes because he remembers the rose bushes at the bottom of the hill.

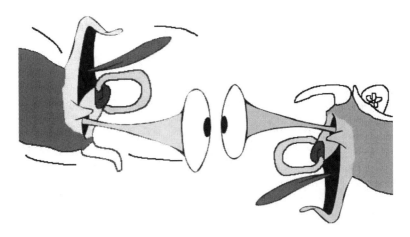

"Oh my," Billy says to himself, "I fell in those just a couple days ago."

Billy was rolling so fast down the hill that all you could see is his eyes in circles on the one side and his bullseye rolling down the hill, like a tire, on the other side.

After landing in the bushes my, my was Billy sore. He limped home with his mother, who ran after to join him.

Once they got home, his mom patched Billy up with lots and lots of Band-Aids all over his body and two BIG ones on the center of his BUTT.

I mentioned that I would tell you about Billy's father. Well, Billy had a father who had a birthmark on his butt just like Billy. Billy wasn't quite sure what happened to his father but it probably had something to do with the bullseye. Some say he might have been part of a knife throwing act at the circus that went horribly wrong.   Others say some whalers mistook him for a bullseye-back-whale and harpooned him, taking his poor father away. But what his mom told him, was that one day while his dad was out grazing in the field an alien spaceship approached earth and seeing this big bullseye in the field, landed on poor Billy's father-- and he was never seen again-- and neither were the aliens, on the account of the explosion.

Belching Bob the Big Bullseye Butt Bull was his name. Some say he ate way too much grass, which made him very fat and made him belch and fart a lot. His wife, Marybelle, didn't have a butt at all, and she didn't fart either, but Bob's butt was huge and more than made up for it, which was why it was a landing strip for aliens. His mother told him the story when he was just a calf, almost with a sense of pride. "Bob saved the world," she would say with a sparkle in her eye and a flutter of her udder.

I wish there was a back story about how Billy fell down all the time, but there isn't. He just fell down all the time and you have to believe me. His friends certainly do.

Anyway, to complete this chapter on Billy falling down, I have to tell you that the next day when Billy went to school with Band-Aids all over his body, all his friends, and even the teacher, laughed at him.

Poor Billy.

2

BILLY'S CHASED BY BEES— OH MY!

One day, while Billy was riding home from school on the school bus, he got off at his stop and started to walk home to his mom. What he didn't realize, or see, was a beehive in the tree above his head full of bees, Killer bees, not like cool bees, but like deadly bees, the Africanized ones, and the hive was starting to come loose. Right as Billy was underneath it, the Beehive fell down and landed right on Billy's head, Kerplop! and Ka-Pow! Bees were swirling around Billy's head inside the hive and stinging him left and right. The bees that were not stinging his face swooped out of the hole on the side of the hive and what did they see-- but his red and white bullseye butt and they flew straight for it.

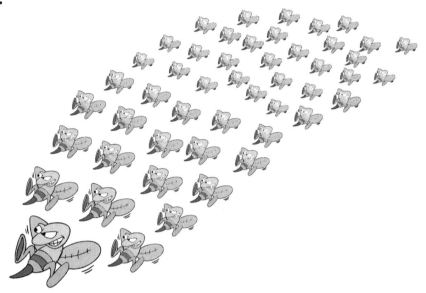

He ran and ran and ran with bees stinging his butt-- and his face. Not seeing where he was running, he turned left and crashed right into the middle of the rose bushes his mom had planted. The very same rose bushes he landed in when he rolled down the hill the week before. The very same rose bushes he fell into right after his mom planted them the month before. See-- Billy falls all the time.

The bees were still stinging, and now the

rose bush thorns were poking Billy here and there, and everywhere. Fortunately the hive got stuck in the rose bushes and came off from his head, but the bees all started after his bullseye. Dazed and confused, Billy limped towards the lake in the back of the yard. Once he got to the lake he jumped in and held his breath under the water where the bees couldn't sting him anymore. He held his breath as long as he could.

He forgot about the bees and they forgot about him, but what he didn't realize, was that there were baby alligators in the lake. Fortunately for Billy they were babies but unfortunately for Billy they still had lots of teeth and were attracted to his bullseye.

They chomped on his legs, and chomped on his hooves, and then chomped on his bullseye butt. Yea-ow! And, when the alligator mom heard all the commotion she came to see what her baby alligators were fussing about, and when she saw the bullseye, she chomped right on his butt. Her teeth were longer than the babies' teeth and the pain made Billy shoot out of the water like a rocket and he landed on the tree in the backyard where still another beehive fell on his head causing Billy to lose his grip and fall down smack on the top of his head-- and the beehive. Billy already couldn't see with his face all swollen up from the last beehive, but even these bees stung his stings, where the other bees stung before, making Billy's swollen face even more swollen, with his eyelids totally clamping shut. Billy couldn't even cry right. He cried so hard from all the pain, water shot out of his nose on account of his eyes being swollen shut. Yeah, his nose. Believe it!

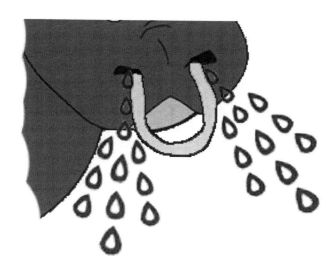

What was Billy to do? He saw stars, he saw butterflies, and he saw bees. Having forgotten about the alligators, 'cause of all the pain, he ran back into the lake and the mama alligator was ready for him this time. That big alligator clamped down again-- 2 times! On his butt!.

This time he flew through the back door into the kitchen. Like all his previous accidents, Marybelle put Band-Aids all over his body and she fed him honey-- something he didn't like to eat anymore.

3

FILBERT THE FUMBLY F☉X CHASES BILLY

One day at the end of school, when Billy was heading home on the school bus, there was no room except for one seat next to Filbert the Fumbly Fox. Filbert was mean and nobody liked him-- not even Billy. Given that the seat next to Filbert was the only space on the bus, and the bus driver didn't let anybody stand up, Billy had no choice but to sit down next to Filbert the Fumbly Fox and take his chances. Billy was safe as they were driving, but when the bus stopped at Billy's house, the bus driver called Billy's named really loud and told him to get out.

Billy got up and started to walk towards the door next to the bus driver, but Filbert got up quickly and pushed Billy to the side and ran past him and through the door, because Filbert was a fox, and he was fast, and he was mean, too. This made Billy so mad that his eyes turned red, and his nostrils flared and steam burst out.

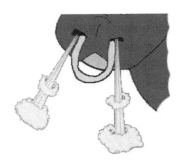

Grunting he ran out as fast as he could to catch Filbert the Fumbly Fox. Billy was so angry, he tripped on the bus step and landed on his chin. When Billy hit the ground, Filbert fell over on his side laughing uncontrollably.

This made Billy even madder and he started to roar towards Filbert jumping the fence in front of his house, bumping the tree, and knocking a beehive from the branches above. The hive broke right behind Billy, fortunately not on his head this time, and unfortunately, the bees getting disturbed from their slumber got angry, too, and started buzzing behind Billy trying to sting him as Billy charged after Filbert. One bee poked Billy, and then another, and then another making Billy run even faster and faster, right past Filbert the Fumbly Fox. Billy had forgotten he was mad because he now hurt really bad.

When Billy ran past Filbert, this time in terror, Filbert saw the bullseye on Billy's Butt and Filbert's eyes widened—"Yippee! I always wanted to play darts. Here I come, ready or not!" said Filbert as he fumbled for his darts that he always carried in his school bag. Once the darts were in his paw, Filbert started chasing Billy right behind the bees, and 1 by 1 "Ee! Owe! Ee!" cried Billy as Filbert kept hitting his butt until there were no more darts.

Filbert wasn't so fumbly after all. After all, he had direct hits. Filbert was having so much fun tormenting Billy with the darts that he got a crazy look in his eyes and decided to sharpen up his teeth and sinking them into Billy's butt.

The bees were stinging Billy and Filbert's darts were stinging Billy, and his teeth chomping on Billy got the bees so scared they decided to fly away and find a new home because Filbert was one scary looking fox.

Poor Billy was getting tired running through the countryside. Tired, barely able to run any longer, not knowing where he was going because it was starting to get dark, Billy finally saw the light on his house porch through the haze of his mind, and headed straight for it. But what Billy didn't remember or see was his mom's rose bushes right in front. Billy ran right through them "Ee! Owe! Ee! Owe!".

Filbert the Fumbly Fox was getting tired too, and running out of steam. When he saw Billy barrel through the rose bushes and scream, Filbert said to himself, "That bull is crazy. I can't follow him into the bushes. That is nutty." So, Filbert went home for supper and Billy finally got away and made it to his house and shut the door as fast as he could.

Bill the Bullseye Butt Bull fell on the couch and took a very long nap. He had forgotten about the thorns and the darts and fell fast asleep. He awoke to extreme pain with his mom Marybelle the Bottomless Butt Bull by his side and pulling the thorns out of his head, his arms, his legs, and it really hurt when she pulled the darts out of his butt. Then she stuck Band-Aids all over his body, AGAIN!

Billy looked like a mummy from Egypt. Tired and sore, Billy went upstairs without dinner and started to walk down the hall. Billy's sister Misty the Sissy Eyed Bull, saw this mummy walking down the hall and screamed hitting him on the head with a hair dryer. Moo! Billy said in pain. Dazed and confused, Billy followed his sister into his bedroom. Full of fright, she had gone the wrong way. She continued to scream but Billy couldn't hear from the hair dryer on his head and he collapsed on his bed. Then the sister saw the big bulls eye from the bandages and laughed. Ha-ha-ha! That's just you Billy.

The next day Billy got up and left for school. He had bandages all over his body, covering his eyes this time, so he had a hard time seeing where is feet were going. On his way to the bus, so he thought, he walked right through the rose bushes again, but this time Billy was so wrapped up in bandages he didn't feel it as much. The Rose thorns hooked on Billy's arms and legs and started to stick everywhere on his legs by the time he got through the rose bushes he looked like a mummy with thorny pants. When his friend Filbert saw Billy approach the bus stop he thought it was a mummy with thorny pants and got scared and started to throw darts at poor Billy to defend himself. Billy got angry and snorted loudly scaring Filbert even more.

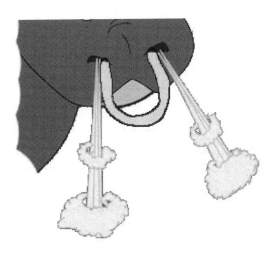

Filbert was nowhere to be seen, so Billy had a nice wait for the bus, but when the bus driver saw a mummy with thorny pants it sped away. Poor Billy had to walk to school with thorns in his pants and gauze all around his body.

When Billy arrived at school, everyone screamed and ran for their lives leaving Billy all alone. The end.

4

CURTIS THE CURLY CACTUS MEETS BILLY ◎

School was coming to a close and Billy was attending his last day. Fortunately, the students were too excited for summer to kick his butt that day. Billy had a great day and was heading home for the summer vacation and when he got home his, mom, Marybelle the Bottomless Butt Bull was so happy to see him. Remember she is called that because she has no butt. Anyway-- She said, "Oh Billy! I'm so glad to see you. we are going to go on a camping trip to celebrate the start of summer." Poor Billy shook in his hooves. He remembered last summer when they went on a boating trip and the captain hooked him on his butt and threw him out to sea. He thought something bad like that was going to happen to him on his camping trip. He hated camping because the mosquitoes, bees, and deerflies would sting him on his butt. Even the porcupines would poke him on his butt because of the target. It was so easy to see— and so-o-o tempting.

What Billy didn't realize was that, this time, they were going to camp in the desert and there were lots and lots of cactus. Billy had only met his mom's rose bushes. He had never met a cactus and I'm sure he had never met a cactus he liked.

After they traveled for hours and hours, and after Billy asked, "Are we there yet—1,000 times," they finally arrived in the middle of the desert, the desert called Death Valley, and set up camp. They arrived so late, they put the tent up by lantern light and poor Billy did not see that Death Valley was full of cactuses. He especially did not see that there was this one cactus that was the meanest of all.

His thorns were curly because he was kind

of crooked. You couldn't trust Curtis the Curly Cactus because he was so mean. Little did Billy know that he would camp right next to Curtis' home and Curtis did not like visitors, especially visitors that were uninvited and unannounced.

Curtis decided to wait 'till morning to make himself known to Billy.

When morning came, Billy went outside his tent to look around and smell the fresh air. When he sat down for breakfast, he ate some eggs unsuspecting what lurked behind him. Suddenly, there was shadow covering his head and then his eggs. He thought to himself, "I thought it was sunny today with no clouds in the sky." Then, the shadow spoke to him. Yikes! Billy almost jumped out of his skin. "You must leave here because this is my home and if you don't leave, you will be pricked from horns to hooves and you will be sorry."

"Who is that?" asked Billy the Bullseye Butt Bull shaking in his hooves. "I am Curtis the Curly Cactus and I am angry." Billy, who had never seen a cactus before in his whole life turned around slowly to see who this menacing voice belonged to. Curtis was 10 feet tall, dark green, and mean.

Curtis asked, "Who are you?" "I am Billy the Bullseye Butt Bull and I am scared," replied Billy. "Why are you angry?"

"I don't like trespassers near my home without permission," cried Curtis.

"Can we stay," begged Billy.

"No!" Cursed Curtis, "Absolutely not!"

"Mama!" bellowed Billy, but there was no answer. Maybelle was out sightseeing. Billy sweat and Billy shook. Then Billy ran!

Curtis saw the red bullseye and his eyes glowed and his thorns grew in the excitement. He bent over as fast as he could and pricked Billy right in the butt. His curly thorns sunk deep, and Curtis sprung back, hurling Billy into the air like a cow flying over the moon landing bullseye first on a sharp, jagged, pointy rock. The agony caused Billy to bounce, landing right next to his mom, with a tear in his eye.

"Momma?" Billy asked. "What is it Poopsie?" Marybelle responded. "Can we go home now?"

But we have only been here a day?

He batted his eyelashes with the cutest tearful face possible.

Then Marybelle conceded, "yes". Do you want to help me pack Billy?

No. I will wait right here where it is safe by the rocks and there is no cactus.

Suit yourself son. I will be right back.

Billy was relieved to be going home. He could handle bees and rose bushes much better than a crooked cactus.

The End

5

DONALD THE FARTING DADDY

Why do Daddy's fart and Mommy's get angry and kids think it's funny?

— 6 —

THE C-B-A's

Who doesn't love the A-B-C's? Savannah, Sierrah, and Daddy named several things that started with each letter. Draw or color these:

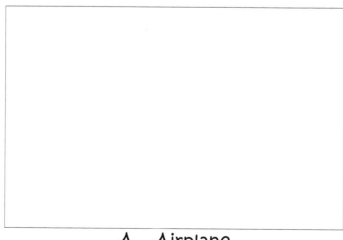

A – Airplane

B – Billy The Bullseye Butt Bull

C – Curtis the Curly Cactus

D – Daddy

E Elephant

F – Filbert the Fumbly Fox

G – Garden

H – House

I – Iguana

J – Jungle

K – Kitten

L – Lollipop

M – Mommy

N – Nutcracker

O – Octopus

P – Porcupine

Q – Quilt

R – Roses

S – Sunflower

T – Turtle

U – Umbrella

V – Violin

W – Waterpark

X – Xylophone

Y – Yellow Submarine

Z – Zebra

And then we sang the song, you know the one:

A   B   C   D   E   F   G

H   I   J   K   L M N O P

And, wouldn't you know it, Sierrah asked Daddy to sing it backwards—so he did.

(If you have trouble reading this, make something up. Have fun!)

?em htiw gnis uoy t'now emit txen

C   B   As ym wonk I won

Z dna Y   X U W

V U T S R Q

P O N M L K J I H

G F E D C B A

You did it!

— 7 —

I WAS A BAD BR⊙THER: ST⊙RY 1 – THE HANDLEBAR "ACCIDENT"

Back when my brother William was 5 and I was 8, we went for a bike ride with our mother. It wasn't as safe in the 1980's. We didn't have to wear bike helmets and I could ride my brother on the handlebars, and it did not alarm our mom at all.

Well, we were riding through our hometown Ramona on B Street and were passing a hardware store. About that time I started to daydream. I daydreamed about the times my brother and I would swing at the park and jump off in mid-air and go flying across the playground, and usually land on our feet. Those were fun times, so I thought maybe if I slam on the breaks, William will go flying and land on his feet. This is what it sort of looked like in my mind.

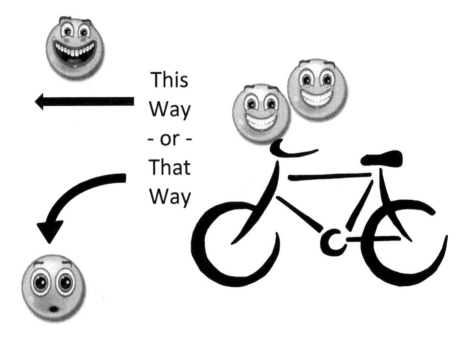

This
Way
- or -
That
Way

Instead, of flying out this way, William flew that way head first right onto the pavement. Within a split second, his head was bleeding and he was dazed and confused. I was surprised. It did not happen how I imagined.

My mom gave me a stern look and said, "what did you do that for?" "I don't know," was all I could think of. Then I blacked out.

— 8 —

I WAS A BAD BR⊚THER: ST⊚RY 2 – WHEELIE C⊚NTEST

If one accident on a bicycle was not enough, then there was two. This one was more painful, and a little less innocent; however, William got much more hurt than intended.

It all started about a year later. William was once injured and twice shy, and now 6 years old. I was 9 and smarter about being a bad brother. William was playing in the back yard and I was playing in the front yard with my friend Sean.

Sean and I were playing with our bicycles and

jumping them off the ridge at the end of the driveway. I got the wonderful idea of having a wheeling contest with my brother... after loosening his handlebars just a little bit.

Like with the slamming of the brakes, I imagined that if I loosened the handlebars just a little bit William would pull a wheelie and land and the bike may turn to the left or the right a little.   Surely you remember when your handlebars were loose and the wheel was out of alignment. It was kind of fun, right?

William's bike was adjusted. I took it for a test-ride and it seemed to work fine. Like I mentioned, not too loose, just a little for fun. With the joke set, I called for William in the back. Sean and I excitedly talked about a wheelie contest, and his head must have hurt, because he said, "No way, I don't trust you." I said, "come on, let me show you," and I took his bike and proceeded to perform a small wheelie at the end of the driveway and ride back. (Like I said, "Not too loose.") William's eyes got as big as saucers and he said, "That was stupid, I can do better than that," and he yanked the bike out of my hands and proceeded to ride all the way to the back of the round driveway to get as much speed as he could. Sean and I looked at each other, and I started to get nervous. As William approached, I said, "Slow Down!" William shouted, "No! I am going to win!" I shouted back, "But you don't have to win." "Yes I do-o-o-o," was the last I heard before this...

William pulled with all his might and the bike went this way and he and the handlebars in his hands went that way. He flew through the air holding the handlebars all the way to the ground. He only let go of one side because that was the side that hit the ground, first.

It looked sort of like this, except William was not smiling, but he was dazed and confused again, but this time extremely angry. This time, there were no parents and I was laughing uncontrollably. It was the funniest thing this 9 year old had ever seen in his entire life. It was an epic fail, but YouTube did not exist at the time. When he came to, he got up and fortunately was so mad he threw the handlebars down, instead of hitting me with them. Instead he charged, but I was a bigger brother, so I stuck my hand out, still laughing, as he swung at me.

I said, "Please calm down. I don't want to hurt you." "Arr, grr, arr," and flailing was all I got, so I lifted my arm and kneed him in the gut. He fell down wriggling in pain long enough to get away.

— 9 —

ONCE UPON A TIME THERE WAS A PRINCESS WHO LIVED IN A BIG CASTLE ON A HILL

Daddy used to always start his bedtime stories like this and then make something up.

Can you make something up to complete the story? I bet you can. The possibilities are limitless.

Once upon a time there was a princess who lived in a big castle on a hill...

DONALD C. KENDIG

10

BURT THE FRIENDLY SPIDER AND FRIENDS

Burt was a spider. He was a garden spider. He was a friendly spider.

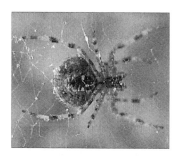

Burt looked very scary, but he wasn't very mean. He was very friendly and he helped keep away the mean mosquitos and the bothersome buzzing flies. Billy the Bullseye Butt Bull liked Burt. No mosquitos meant no itchy bumps on his butt and no flies meant no having to swat his butt with his tail.

Burt had a wide variety of friends and relatives. Not all of them were nice, some of them were naughty, and some of them were downright dangerous. I will list Burt's naughty, nice, and dangerous friends here. You can add some of your own and you can practice looking them up on the Internet.

Naughty! ! !
- Gary the Gopher Snake
- Beatrice the Bee
- Alex the Aphid
- Barry the Black Ant
- Candice the Caterpillar

- _____
- _____
- _____

Nice ☺ ☺ ☺
- Terrance the Tarantula

- Bonnie the Butterfly
- Maurice the Moth
- Lula the Ladybug
- Roger the Rollie-Pollie

- _____

- _____

- _____

Dangerous ☹ ☹ ☹
- Beulah the Black Widow
- Sid the Scorpion
- Randy the Red Ant
- Wanda the Wasp
- Richard the Rattlesnake

- _____

- _____

- _____

- _____

DONALD C. KENDIG

AB◉UT THE AUTH◉R

Donald C. Kendig, father of two beautiful daughters, Savannah and Sierrah, had no idea what he had in store when he finally decided that, "this was the time for children" and his wife said, "I'm pregnant!" Having struggled in English in both grade-school and high-school, he acquired a talent for writing by grading his "wife-to-be's" term papers, writing numerous news articles for college and his homeowners association, and drafting hundreds, if not thousands, of emails and memos in the first 18 years of his working career. Storytelling was never his strong suit, but, "My girls made me do it" and they made him do it at all hours of the night when he had come home from a long day and could barely keep his eyes straight let alone his thinking. Girls are like boys, and like all kids, like stories about castles, kingdoms, farting, chasing something, getting hurt, sibling rivalry, pranks, and butts, with characters that have funny names. "I hope I have been a good father." Time will tell.

Made in the USA
Middletown, DE
17 July 2016